LEAVE ME ALONE!

Vera Brosgol

Roaring Brook Press
New York

Once there was an old woman.
She lived in a small village in a
small house . . .

. . . with a very big family.

Winter was coming.

That meant she had some very important knitting to do.

But it wasn't getting done.

Her grandchildren were very
curious about her knitting:

Were you supposed to hit
the ball with a stick?

Could you eat it?

Could you make your
brother eat it?

Why did the ball get smaller
and smaller as you chased it?

The old woman was at
the end of her rope.

So she made her bed as neatly as she could.

She swept the floorboards until they more or less shone.

She drank tea from her samovar.

She packed up her things in a big sack,
and as she left she shouted back . . .

The old woman walked through the deep, dark forest.

She made a fire so that she could see what she was doing.

Then she sat down and began to knit.

The bear family was very curious
about the light from her fire . . .
and about what she might taste like.

Leave Me Alone!

the old woman shouted.

But they didn't listen, because bears don't speak English.

So she picked up her sack and left.

The old woman climbed up
the mountainside.

It was cold, so she found
a small sheltered place.

Then she sat down
and began to knit.

The mountain goats were excited to have a visitor.

Especially one that brought snacks!

the old woman
shouted.

But the goats were too busy fighting over the red ones, which they all agreed were the best.

So she picked up her sack and left.

The old woman
climbed higher
and higher up the
mountain.

She reached the
top and climbed
onto the moon.

She found a rock that was
shaped like a chair.

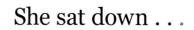

She sat down . . .

and began to knit.

The little green moon-men had never seen a woman before, old or otherwise. They examined her with handheld scanners that went "beep boop."

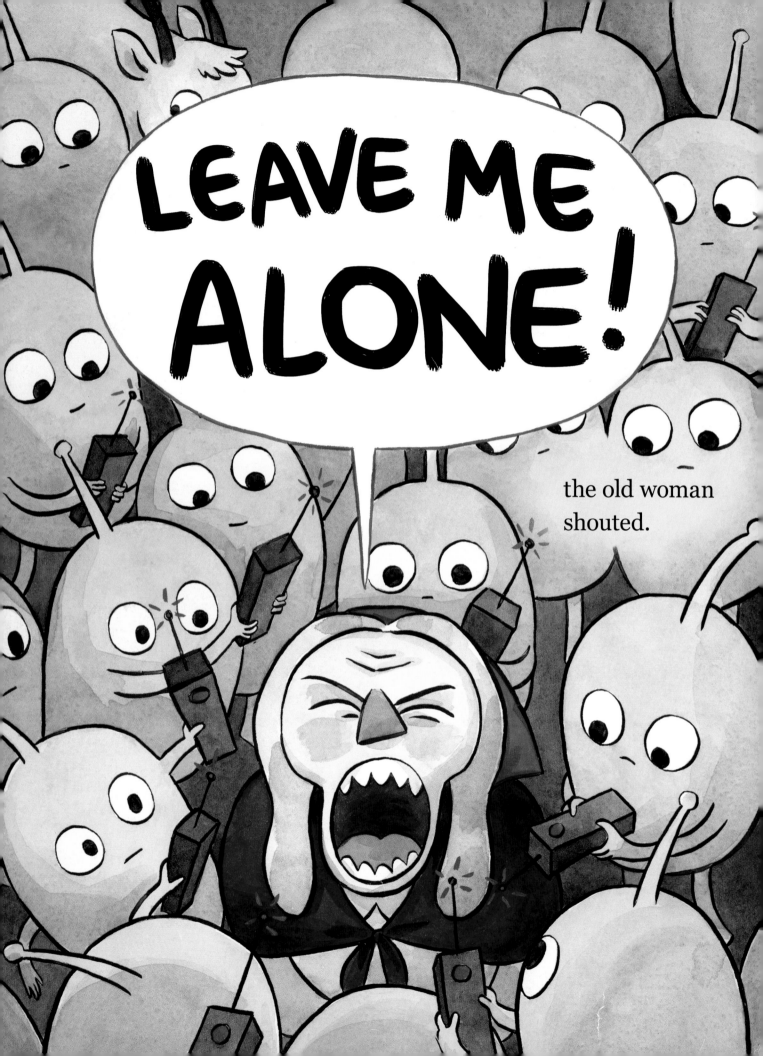

But the little green moon-men
couldn't hear her, because they
didn't have any ears.

So she picked up her
sack and left through
a wormhole.

The void on the other side of the
wormhole was very dark and
very, very quiet.

She was absolutely,
completely,
utterly
alone.

It was PERFECT.

Soon she had no more yarn
and thirty little sweaters.

And she was alone.

So she put the thirty sweaters into her big sack.

She swept the void until it was a nice, matte black.

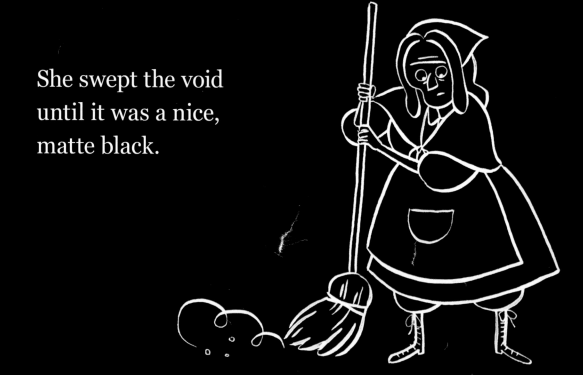

She had a cup of tea
from her samovar.

Then she picked up the sack and
left through another wormhole.

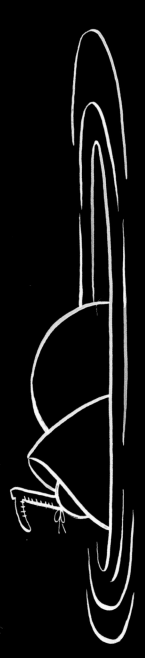

When she came out the other side, everything was right where she'd left it.

And she didn't say a word.

For Jeremy

Copyright © 2016 by Vera Brosgol
Published by Roaring Brook Press
Roaring Brook Press is a division of Holtzbrinck Publishing Holdings Limited Partnership
175 Fifth Avenue, New York, New York 10010
mackids.com

Library of Congress Cataloging-in-Publication Data
Names: Brosgol, Vera, author, illustrator.
Title: Leave me alone / Vera Brosgol.
Description: First edition. | New York : Roaring Brook Press, 2016. |
   Summary: Grandmother wants so badly to be left alone to finish the
   knitting for her grandchildren that she leaves her tiny home and her big
   family to journey to the moon and beyond to find peace and quiet to finish
   her knitting.
Identifiers: LCCN 2016002024 | ISBN 9781626724419 (hardback)
Subjects: | CYAC: Grandmothers—Fiction. | Knitting—Fiction. |
   Solitude—Fiction. | Picture books. | BISAC: JUVENILE FICTION / Humorous
   Stories. | JUVENILE FICTION / Family / Multigenerational. | JUVENILE
   FICTION / Family / General (see also headings under Social Issues).
Classification: LCC PZ7.1.B788 Le 2016 | DDC [E]—dc23
LC record available at https://lccn.loc.gov/2016002024

Our books may be purchased in bulk for promotional, educational,
or business use. Please contact your local bookseller or the Macmillan Corporate
and Premium Sales Department at (800) 221-7945 ext. 5442 or by e-mail at
MacmillanSpecialMarkets@macmillan.com.

First edition 2016
Book design by Andrew Arnold
Printed in the United States of America by Worzalla,
Stevens Point, Wisconsin

3   5   7   9   10   8   6   4